I0757477

ISBN 978-0-578-45918-9

"To my beloved mama Alicia, who never stopped believing in me. May you fly high with the angels." - A.P.

Our plane prepares to land, and boy, am I excited!
The first thing I see is the big blue ocean
surrounding the city we're headed to!

My name is Agustina, and I can't wait to bring you on this adventure.
I bet you're wondering where I'm going. Take a guess!
I'll give you a hint: I'm somewhere in Mexico.

I am in the city of Veracruz!

My parents call it la ciudad mas bella, which means
"the most beautiful city."

My parents travel here often to visit my abuelita
and some of my extended family.
This is my and Guillermo's first time in the beautiful city.

Veracruz is a city in the state of Veracruz in Mexico. Doesn't make sense?
Think of it like New York city,
it's a city in the state of New York in the United States.

The city of Veracruz has been around for centuries.
Spanish settlers discovered the city long ago
when they were on a grand mission!

Some say the explorers were on the lookout for
gold when they found the city.
Maybe they were pirates! Spending time here will sure be a ton of fun!

Our first stop is Playa Villa Del Mar!
We're going for a swim! Splash!
I love the sound the waves make.

The water is so clear.
I can even see my magenta pink toe nails through the water!

Guess where we're going to next?!
To the Veracruz Aquarium! We're going to have a magnificent time.
I can't wait to see all kinds of sea animals from different parts of the world.
Turtles, jellyfish, penguins and even toucans!

Right when we walk in, we see a gigantic shark!

His teeth look mighty sharp and scary.
Guillermo points out how impressive his fins look when he swims.

The Aquarium is extraordinary!
It's interesting visiting an aquarium in another country.
I'm excited to see what else Veracruz has in store for us tomorrow!

Veracruz has one of the largest ports in Mexico, and many ships stop here.
My family and I take a stroll along a waterfront promenade known as El Malecón.
We watch as some ships unload and others go.

It's nice to take in how beautiful Veracruz truly is...

Every year the city has a big carnival. My parents say it's a tradition! The carnival has music, all types of food, and a spectacular event...

What is that spectacular event, you ask? A parade!
The parade has enormous floats, marching bands, and incredible dancers.

Guillermo and I are so excited!

Our parents have been talking about the carnival since we got here!

As the parade begins, we're amazed by all the dazzling colors we see.
Violet, scarlet, sapphire!
The parade is truly a masterpiece.

Oh! And we can't forget about the delicious Mexican cuisine!

My abuelita says the tamales in Veracruz are tasty and mouthwatering!

I'm trying my very first today. I take one bite, and boy, is she right!

It's warm, mushy and delicious!

But I also love Veracruz's sweets! Pan dulce is my favorite!
It is sweet tasty bread served in Mexico and other Latin countries.

Veracruz also has a ton of panaderias. A panaderia is a bakery.
My parents are taking us to a well known panaderia
that has all sorts of warm yummy pasteries.

We get there and oh my!
I can't help but glance over the rows of galletas grajeas and bolillos.
They look fresh out of the oven, and so colorful!

Guillermo gets a sugar covered churro, and I get a delicious galleta grajea.

Our last stop is La Laguna de Mandinga!
Guillermo, my parents, and I will be taking a boat ride around a lagoon!

The scenery is astounding, and the sunset is spectacular!
It feels as if we're going on an adventurous boat ride in a tropical rainforest.

Veracruz has been a ton of fun!

I cannot wait to come again! We've had such a fantastic time.
From the amazing culture to the beautiful scenery.

Until next time, friends!
We might go to another magnificent country, and I might just be your tour guide!
Adios!

Alice Perez is a primary school teacher and a children's book author. Perez is a Texas native, born and raised in Houston.

She has always had a passion for storytelling and writing. Perez wrote her first story at the early age of ten for a fourth grade class project. When the assignment was given, she was thrilled because she had an opportunity to express her love for writing. Little did she know that this would be the beginning of her own story.

Perez's goal is to bring diversity to children's books. She hopes to write more books about cities in different countries and take young readers on adventures around the world through her writings.

Milica Colic is an illustrator and graphic designer from Belgrade, Serbia. The young artist holds a bachelor's degree in graphic design and a master's in computer science.

Colic's passion for art began at a young age. She recalls having an interest in art since the first time she held a pen. In 2018, Colic took on the opportunity to work with Perez on "Vamos a Veracruz", and together they created Agustina, the main character of Perez's premier book.

This is the first time Colic's vibrant illustrations have been featured in a children's book.